TWISTED JUSTICE

TWISTED JUSTICE

a Mecana Novella

JOHN L. LANSDALE

BookVoice Publishing 2018

Twisted Justice © Copyright 2018
by John L. Lansdale
All rights reserved.

Cover design © Copyright 2018
All rights reserved.

Interior design Copyright © 2018
by BookVoice Publishing
All rights reserved.

ISBN
978-1-949381-03-0 Paperback
978-1-949381-02-3 eBook

BookVoice Publishing
PO Box 1528
Chandler, TX 75758
www.bookvoicepublishing.com

THE MECANA SERIES by John L. Lansdale
#1 - Horse of a Different Color
#2 - When the Night Bird Sings
#3 - Twisted Justice

Titles by John L. Lansdale
Slow Bullet
Long Walk Home
Zombie Gold
The Last Good Day
Broken Moon
Shadows West (with Joe R. Lansdale)
Hell's Bounty (with Joe R. Lansdale)
Boy and Hog (Short Story)
Boy and Hog Return (Short Story)
Emergency Christmas (Short Story)
Tales from the Crypt (Comic Series)
That Hellbound Train (Graphic Novel)
Yours Truly, Jack the Ripper (Graphic Novel)
Shadow Warrior (Graphic Novel)
Justin Case (Graphic Novel)

Follow the author online at
www.bookvoicepublishing.com
www.twitter.com/mybookvoice
www.goodreads.com/johnllansdale
www.facebook.com/bookvoicepublishing

<u>What Others are Saying about John L. Lansdale</u>

A "page-turner...Lansdale effectively delays revealing the novel's big secret until the end. Those who like their thrillers with a heavy dose of violent action will be satisfied."
– *Publishers Weekly* review of **Slow Bullet**

"This is an entertaining, science fiction-historical-horror blend with resourceful protagonists and a solid cast of secondary characters." – *Booklist* review of **Zombie Gold**

"The author's innate ability to spin a complex tale painted with vivid characters and intense suspense provides readers with a well-paced book that they may find difficult to set down...a worthwhile suspenseful ride."
– *Amazing Stories* review of **Horse of a Different Color**

"A straight-ahead thriller…it's about action, and there's plenty of that. Check it out."
– *Bill Crider's Pop Culture Magazine* review of **Slow Bullet**

"Has something for everyone… It's exciting, entertaining and educational. A fun ride."
– TV personality Joan Hallmark review of **Zombie Gold**

"Something unique and comfortable and difficult to put down. Highly recommended."
– *Cemetery Dance* review of **Hell's Bounty**

"True to Lansdale tradition, John L. Lansdale has compiled a piece of work that should appeal to a wide range of readers." – *Amazing Stories* review of **Zombie Gold**

*For Keith and Kasey,
and of course always Mary*

*Day before yesterday comes the day
After tomorrow every day.*
- Author

PROLOGUE

As a parade of speakers put in their two cents at Robert Verves' retirement ceremony, he watched his daughter and wife glancing at him as every speaker from the Mayor on down gave him praise for his long career and all his heroic accomplishments. When they called his daughter for her turn he thought about her as a little girl, when she was the furthest thing from his mind one Sunday morning in 1989.

THIRTY YEARS AGO

Two men dressed in black entered the dark kitchen of a small house in a suburb of Dallas, Texas. Both men were holding automatics with silencers at the ready. Three rows of cut cocaine with straws and a razor blade lay on the kitchen table. One of the men stopped and took a quick snort of cocaine, shook his head, and followed the other man to a staircase. They tiptoed up the stairs to a partially open bedroom door where a thirty-something Mexican man and woman lay sleeping. Without a word the men pointed pistols at them. The bullets made a whiffing sound as several rounds found their mark in each body. A little girl sleeping at the foot of the bed never woke up and was spared for whatever reason. One of the men picked up a briefcase from a night table, snapped it open, nodded to the other man, closed it, and they retreated down the stairs and left the way they entered.

An insomniac from the next door saw the two strangers running from the house and called the police. The little toddler was still sleeping early Sunday morning when detectives Robert Verves and his partner Simon Necessary from the Dallas Police Department entered the bedroom with guns drawn.

The two cops had been partners for three years and were considered the odd couple of the department. Both were in their early thirties. Robert Verves was black a former navy seal. His wife ran a mail order business from their home. They had no kids. Simon on the other hand was white, thin and balding with big blue eyes. He had never served in the military and was considered a bit of a nerd with a master's degree in criminal justice. His wife was a practicing attorney who some how found time to have four kids.

"Looks like they're Mexican," Robert said.

"No shit," Simon said. "You could tell that right away?"

"One of these days… wham! boom! right in the kisser," Robert said.

"You wouldn't hit a superior officer would you," Simon said and put his finger on his badge.

"Just because you've got a lower number don't mean nothing. I might enjoy it. I'm going to get the girl out of here before I decide to do that."

"Good idea" Simon said.

Robert picked up the little girl and carried her downstairs. Simon remained in the room waiting for the crime lab guys.

The little girl opened her eyes, saw Robert, made a horrible face and began to scream.

"What's your name honey?" he asked.

The little girl continued to cry and struggled to pull free of his grasp.

"It's okay, sweetheart, I'm not going to hurt you. You can't see mommy and daddy."

Simon thundered down the stairs. "What the hell are you doing, you're scaring her to death."

"Nothing, I can't let her go up there. I was trying to find out her name."

"She's barely big enough to walk. She sure isn't going to outrun you. See if there's a bottle in the fridge."

"What kind of bottle?"

"A baby bottle, dumbass. Surely they have one."

"I don't know anything about babies. You're the one with all the kids," Verves said.

"I'll loan you some," Simon said.

"No thanks, they look too much like you."

"Never mind", Simon said. "Watch her, I'll go get it."

Simon returned with a bottle of milk with a nipple on it. She looked at it but didn't move.

"Leche, it's leche," Simon said, thrusting the bottle toward her.

The little girl looked at Simon for a second, took the bottle and stuck the nipple in her mouth.

"Como te llama?" Simon asked.

"Sunda," the little girl said.

"Your name is Sunday?" Robert said.

"I think she's trying to say Sandra," Simon said.

"I don't know," Robert said. "Sounds more like Sunday."

"Who would name their baby Sunday?"

"I would," Robert said. "It's pretty cool."

"Some people shouldn't have kids," Simon said. "The child services lady will be here soon, let her figure it out. I'm going back upstairs to look for evidence. With that coke in the house, most likely something they did or didn't do over drugs."

"You could tell that right away?" Robert said, eyeing Simon.

"Okay, we're even," Simon said and hurried back up the stairs.

"I'll call the narcs."

Later that afternoon, detectives Verves and Necessary were sitting at a desk gulping down coffee, trying to piece together the case when the telephone rang.

Robert answered it and switched on the speaker phone.

"This is Cummings at the lab. I hope you appreciate us coming in on a Sunday."

"What do you think we're doing, having a party?" Robert said.

"Probably," Cummings said. "We got some prints we matched up. The border patrol had a make on them. It looks like they were here illegally. Border Patrol sent them back to Mexico about six months ago. The man is Jose Ramirez and the woman Maria Estella. No one has claimed the bodies, probably afraid of being arrested."

"What about the baby?" Robert asked.

"Far as we know she's their kid. She has the same O blood type as both of them."

"Who's got the baby?" Robert said.

"She's at the hospital being checked out."

"Thanks," Robert said. "Do some leg work for us and see what you come up with."

"I'll send you a report."

"Thanks," Robert said and hung up.

"We might as well go home, get some rest and start checking the neighborhood in the morning," Simon said.

"Sounds good to me," Robert said.

When Robert told his wife Valisa about the toddler she asked what was going to happen to her.

"I don't know, they're checking for relatives. Seems her parents were drug mules for the cartel and must've made the wrong people mad. She's being taken care of by Child Protective Services. The assumption right now is she's a Mexican national."

"Why didn't you ask if we could keep her until they find a place for her?" Valisa said.

"It never occurred to me. I should have guessed. You take in every stray in town."

"You think they will find any relatives?" she said.

"I don't know, but I do know what's running through your head. I know we've been talking about adopting a baby but it's not likely they would let us have her, even if they can't find any kin. She's Mexican, we're black and we don't speak Spanish."

"How much Spanish could she know? You said a toddler - that means she doesn't know many words. I wouldn't think that would be a problem."

"You're really thinking about checking this out, aren't you?" Robert said.

Valisa nodded and smiled. She was pretty with big sparkling brown eyes, a good figure and a sense of humor. She and Robert had been married since they were teenagers. Unfortunately she couldn't have kids as a result of a battle with cancer.

"Won't hurt to check it out," Valisa said. "She needs a home and you know people at CPS."

"Yes I do, but I don't think I have any influence. We'll probably have to stay on the adoption list until it's our time."

"Maybe not if you use your connections. Get Simon to help you, he knows everybody."

"That he does. I'll see what I can do, but you haven't even seen this baby."

"Is she healthy, bright?"

"Yes, very."

"Then I want to help her."

With some help from Simon's connections, and a little bit of cheating the system, Robert and his wife were granted temporary custody of the baby.

A year later, the only thing the police came up with was a midwife named Juanita Gonzales who said she delivered the baby in Brownsville, Texas on Christmas Eve 1984, and signed a notarized affidavit that would make the baby a U.S. citizen. The midwife said Maria told her the child's father was a very important rich American she was a nanny for, but didn't give a name. No one bothered to change the records to show that the man Maria was killed with was not the child's father.

A year later, when the case had gone cold and no one had showed to claim her, the Verves were given permanent custody of the girl.

The adoption clerk asked her name and Robert replied, "Mostly just baby girl. We didn't know we would get to keep her. I think she said her name was Sunday or Sandra."

"Okay Sandra," the clerk said. "What's the middle name?"

"No wait, how about Sunday Morning? That's when I found her. It has a good ring to it".

The clerk shook his head. "Heaven help her," he said and filled in the name.

She was officially Sunday Morning Verves.

PRESENT DAY

She was all grown up now, standing at the podium wearing her police uniform, telling everyone about her dad and nothing about how she became Sunday Morning Verves.

CHAPTER 1

It was official – Robert Verves was retired.

He even left a daughter on the force to carry on for him.

His comrades were congratulating him when he noticed Thomas Mecana standing with his new bride Darcie Connors, just back from their honeymoon. Mecana's friend and best man DeMax was also standing with the newlyweds.

"Well, what're you going to do now, Chief?" Mecana said as they shook hands.

"Guess me and Valisa will travel. Maybe I'll build some things for the house."

DeMax walked up to the chief and shook his hand. "Never thought I would be around so many policemen who weren't after me."

"Never thought you would be a detective with Mecana either," Verves said.

"Me neither," DeMax said.

Darcie hugged Robert's neck. "Congratulations. You need us, call anytime," she said.

"Thanks. I will," he said.

Simon Necessary was the new Chief of Homicide and only a step away from retiring himself.

Sunday Morning Verves had grown into a beautiful woman with sparkling brown eyes, shiny midnight hair and curves like a mountain road. She was a Spanish beauty with a very limited Spanish vocabulary. She sat her coffee cup down on her desk and picked up a homicide report. The primary suspect listed Simon Necessary's daughter Angela as his employer. Angela owned one of the best restaurants in town and was on a well-deserved vacation to Cancun with her boyfriend.

Sunday picked up the report and took it to Simon, who was opening a bottle of Tums. The short, once-thin-framed thirty-five-year-old of twenty-five years ago was now a two hundred pound fat guy with a bald head.

Simon took a couple of tablets from the bottle, tossed them in his mouth and started chewing. "What you got, Sunday?"

"I was looking through this drug dealer's murder file and saw Angela's name listed as the suspect's employer," Sunday said.

"Yeah I know. She told me about it. She hired him a couple of months ago. She was desperate for a cook and didn't check him out. He must have had a falling out with his supplier and they put a bullet in his head."

"You know I have to talk to Angela about this when she gets back."

"I know. Do your job. I'm sure she doesn't know anything about it other than what she told me, but you got to do what you got to do. Call her if you think you should."

"No, that's not necessary," she said, paused and looked at Simon. "I think I just made a joke."

"Get that kind of thing all the time." Simon said.

"I'll make sure she doesn't have to answer questions from anyone else when she gets back."

"Thanks. How's your dad handling his retirement?"

"Not too good. He's driving Mom crazy hanging around the house all the time. Doesn't know what to do with himself."

"That's why I keep putting it off. The only life I know is this and raising kids, and all the kids are gone. Angela's the only one who isn't married. Although that might change while she and Doug are in Mexico."

Sunday smiled "She and I had a bet when we were in college about who was going to be the first to get married and have babies. Look's like it's a Mexican standoff, if you will pardon my pun. I'm full of them today."

"Kind of. You know don't you?" Simon said.

"Yes, Mom told me years ago. We just didn't tell Dad I knew until I was in college. Afraid he was the one who couldn't handle it. Then he told me the full story. I'm a lucky woman."

"They love you very much," Simon said. "You need to find you a steady boyfriend."

"Too busy," she said.

"All work and no play will make Sunday a dull girl."

"I think I'm already there. Maybe I'll get around to it if I find someone I have a special justerest in."

"I hope it's soon so I can be the godfather."

"Don't hold your breath," she said. "I've got to get back to work."

"Yeah, me too. I'm never going to eat pizza again," Simon said, reaching for more Tums.

"Famous last words," Sunday said.

CHAPTER 2

After work, Sunday stopped by her parents' house to check on them. No one knew except Valisa and Sunday that Robert had retired because of heart problems, not because he wanted to.

She parked, unlocked the front door, walked in and called out for someone to let them know she was in the house. Robert was a little jumpy when he heard a noise he couldn't see or recognize.

Valisa walked in the room. "Hi sugar," she said. "I haven't seen you in a week."

"I've been real busy, Mom. Where's Dad?"

"He's in his workshop. He thinks he's building a table I want. I don't, but I won't tell him. It gives him something to do."

"He doing alright, taking his medicine?"

"Yes, he's just bored. Building a table is not as exciting as chasing a bad guy."

"How about you?" Sunday asked.

"I'm fine. You want to stay for dinner?"

"No, I think I'll go home, put a TV dinner in the microwave, take me a hot bath and watch Law and Order."

"You sound like your dad. You live and breathe that job. You need to find you a boyfriend"

"That's what Simon said."

"He's right. You should get a roommate or move back home."

"I thought you didn't approve of living together before marriage."

"You know what I meant; a female roommate."

"Nowadays you don't know, Mom." Sunday batted her eyes and gave her mom a hug. "I'll say hello to Dad then go."

Robert was measuring the tabletop when she walked in. He set his tape measure down and hugged her. "Baby girl, I miss you," he said.

"I do you too, Dad. Mom said you were building her a table?"

"Trying to."

"Dad, I need to ask you something."

"Shoot," he said.

"I've been working on a case you probably heard about. It's the guy that supposedly killed a drug dealer last week?"

"Yeah, I heard. Are you getting anywhere?"

"Angela is listed in the report as the suspect's employer. Simon knows that. What I didn't tell him was the guy told his lawyer Angela was supplying him with the drugs. You know how I feel about drug dealers."

"You should forget it. Have you talked to her?"

"No, not yet. I was waiting for her to get back from vacation. I thought I should give her the benefit of the doubt."

"That's the right thing to do. He's just running his mouth, trying to blame someone else for his problems. I can't imagine Angela being mixed up in anything like that."

"Me neither, but I talked to one of her employees and she said some guy she didn't know dropped off Brad's car at the restaurant and said he wanted it serviced before they went on vacation. Big Dog Lopez was with him, too."

"It could have been loaded with money going to Mexico," Robert said.

"The question is: if it was, did Angela know?" Sunday said. "I'm wondering how I should handle it."

"You know much about the boyfriend?" Robert asked.

"No, I only met him once. I know he's a lawyer."

"Might be something you should check out."

"I'm waiting on a report," she said.

"Follow your nose and work the case the way you would any investigation. Find the truth. Lopez is a lowlife but until you have the facts do like you said. Don't jump to conclusions."

"I've got a bad feeling about this," Sunday said. "The truth might be something none of us want to hear."

"You can't help that. The facts won't change and you have no other recourse. Work the case and don't worry about the fallout. You're a good detective. Do your job."

"That's what Simon said."

"He means it, whatever the circumstances. I just hope there's nothing that will hurt him."

"Me too," Sunday said. "I have to go. I'll say goodbye to mom. Thanks for the advice, it helps. Take care of yourself."

"I'll do that baby girl."

When Sunday got home she did exactly what she said she would do, but the episode of Law and Order was a rerun. She couldn't help worrying about Angela. She knew she was having money problems. The restaurant wasn't doing the business it had been doing and she was having trouble making payroll and keeping the restaurant afloat. Surely she wouldn't resort to getting involved with drug dealers. Or would she?

She lay down on the couch and tried to watch Law and Order to get her mind off Angela and went to sleep. She woke up at three in the morning, turned the TV off and went to bed. She had difficulty going back to sleep, thinking about Angela and their college days together and knew she wouldn't rest until she found out what Angela was doing. Was it right or wrong?

CHAPTER 3

On the way to work the next morning, Sunday was wondering how she was going to tell Simon she thought Angela may be involved with drug dealers. There was no good way to do it.

When she walked in the building there was a TV crew and several reporters in Simon's office. Eddy Hanson, Sunday's partner on the occasional assignment, was sitting at his desk, looking at all the fuss going on.

"What's all this about?" she asked him.

"Mexican police found Angela's boyfriend Doug dead in a Juarez alleyway last night. Angela and the car are missing. They didn't even make it five miles into Mexico before it happened."

"Oh no," Sunday said.

Simon came storming out of his office with people following.

"Get the hell out of here and leave me alone! Don't you have any respect for my family? I'll give you a statement when I'm ready, now leave me alone." He turned and retreated back into his office and slammed the door.

Sunday walked to the closed door and tapped on it. "Can I come in? It's Sunday."

"Yeah, come on in." Simon was sitting at his desk, head in hands, tears streaming down his face.

She closed the door and stood there in silence for a few moments while he tried to get himself together. "I'm so sorry, Simon. What can I do?"

"Nothing. We don't have any jurisdiction down there," Simon said. "They asked me to stay here for now. They'll ship Doug's body to his family. All I can do is wait. I don't understand why they were driving to Mexico They were supposed to fly. Juarez police found Doug sometime after three this morning dead. They said he still had his wallet and his Rolex on his wrist. Angela's purse was laying next to him with all its contents, money, cards, everything. That's how they knew she was missing and called the El Paso police. Whoever killed him left the things so everyone would know it was just about a killing, nothing else."

"Simon, I was having a hard time trying to tell you Angela may be involved with drug dealers to save her restaurant and this is what it's all about. I'm having a report run on Doug. I'll let you know what I come up with."

"Something I should have done. I have to go home and be with my family and decide what to do now."

"Of course, I understand. I'm so sorry. I had to tell you about the drugs."

"You had to tell the truth as you saw it." Simon got up gave Sunday a hug.

"I'm here if you need me," she said.

Simon nodded, and walked out.

Sunday stood there looking at all the awards he had on the wall. He deserved better than this, she thought. She walked back out of his office to Hanson's desk.

"Eddy, I'm going to pay a visit to Big Dog. Call Juarez PD and see if they know anything about Angela."

"I don't think they'll tell us anything," Eddy said. "I'll go with you."

"No, I'll call if I need back up. Make the call. If they don't know, I know someone who can find out."

"Who's that?" Eddy asked.

"Thomas Mecana."

"He's probably all out of favors," Eddie said.

"His new wife Darcie is a good friend of mine. We worked together in the civil department a few years back. She was a good lawyer and I grew up with Mecana around. I'll call him, you call Mexico."

CHAPTER 4

Sunday pulled up to the curb in front of Shooters Pool Hall. Two young muscled-up guys with dreadlocks walked up beside her car. The bigger of the two stuck his leg between the door and the car before she could close the door.

"Hey pretty mama," he said. "Want to party?"

"I'm looking for Big Dog," she said and pulled her jacket back to show them her badge. "I hear he hangs out here."

The big guy pulled his leg back and they both stepped up on the sidewalk.

"Man, man, what a waste," the smaller one said.

"Get out of my way," Sunday said.

"Don't get your panties in a bunch, lady," the little one said and stepped out of her way.

"Might be in there," the big one said, pointing at the pool hall door. "No guarantee you'll come out if you go in, though."

"You two go first," Sunday said.

The two walked in with Sunday following. Big Dog Lopez was shooting pool and drinking a beer, his long hair flopping on his head, wearing a gold chain with links the size of a bicycle chain around his neck.

"This cop says she needs to have a talk with you," the tall one said. "Don't think it's about where you go to church."

"You know Angela Necessary?" Sunday asked.

"You're kidding. Her name's Necessary?"

"Got a witness that saw you with the guy who brought her fiancé's car to her restaurant. Somebody murdered her boyfriend down in Mexico, and now she and the car are missing."

"I don't know what you're talking about," Big Dog said.

"I think you do. Why were you in the car?"

"I got nothing to say to you, cop."

"Don't play games with me, asshole. Do you know her?" Sunday said.

"No," Big Dog said and shot the eight ball in a side pocket.

The pool hall door swung open and Mecana and DeMax walked in.

"Mecana," Sunday said. "What a surprise. I was going to call you."

"Eddy called, said Angela was missing and you went to see Big Dog. I hauled this scumbag in several times when I was a cop," Mecana said and turned to Big Dog. "You know anything about the missing woman, shitface?"

"You think I'm psychic?" Big Dog said.

"I think you're going to be dog meat if you don't tell her," DeMax said. He picked the cue stick up off the table and slammed it into the back of Big Dog's legs. He fell to the floor with a yell, shook his head and looked at DeMax.

"What'd you do that for, you sonofabitch?" Big Dog said, rubbing his legs. "I'm goin' to get you for that."

"Don't fuck with us," DeMax said. "Biggen, you and Squirt stay out of it."

Big Dog looked at Sunday. "We got rights too."

"Stay where you are, Big Dog," Mecana said. "And you two, put your hands on the pool table where I can see them."

"Why are you doing this, Mecana, you're not a cop," Big Dog said.

"I just don't like you," Mecana said.

"Tell me why you were with the driver or I'll turn DeMax loose on you again," Sunday told Big Dog.

"Just riding with my buddy."

"You're admitting you were there," Sunday said.

"Yeah, so what," Big Dog said.

DeMax kicked Big Dog's leg sideways and stepped on his knee. He yelled again and rolled over on the floor.

"What happened to you, dickhead, you get religion?" Big Dog said.

"Tell her what she wants to know," DeMax said. "Or I'm going to break both your legs."

"I don't know what happened to her. I was just helping a friend."

"You have any names?" Mecana said.

"My friend Miguel was the driver. That's all I know."

"What's his last name," Mecana said.

"We don't ever give each other last names," Big Dog said, rubbing his knee.

"I think you should go ahead and break his legs, DeMax," Mecana said.

"Okay," DeMax said and moved toward Big Dog.

"I don't know her," Big Dog said.

"But you knew what was going to happen."

"No."

"Bullshit," Mecana said.

"What about you two?" Sunday asked.

"Nah, we don't know nothing," Squirt said.

"Put your hands behind your back, Big Dog, you're under arrest," Sunday said.

"What for?"

"You're a murder suspect," Sunday said. "I'll have someone pick up your buddy. Maybe he knows something useful."

DeMax stood Big Dog up and grabbed his arms behind his back as Sunday put the cuffs on.

Sunday walked Big Dog out to her car and slammed the door.

"Where's Darcie at?" she asked Mecana.

"Waiting on furniture to be delivered to our new house," Mecana said. "We sold the old place and found a nice one in a good neighborhood. Anything you need me to do?"

"If I go to Mexico the department will drown me in red tape, and if Angela's not dead by now she definitely will be by the time we get approval to go."

"It could be a year," Mecana said. "Eddy told us what happened. Me and DeMax can take a ride down to Mexico."

"I can get you expense money but that's about it," Sunday said.

"I don't need it. I owe your dad for what he's done for me. Where's the last place she was seen alive?"

"On the Mexican side of El Paso in Juarez," Sunday said.

Biggen and Squirt opened the pool hall door and stepped out onto the street next to Sunday's car. "We'll get you out," Biggen yelled at Big Dog.

"I don't think so," Sunday said. "Go on before I take you in, too."

Biggen and Squirt waved at Big Dog as two more of his friends came out of the pool hall and stood in front of Sunday's car.

"Get you ass away from the car," DeMax said to the two guys and they slowly walked away. "Let's get out of here."

"I'll lock up Big Dog and buy you lunch at Brogans before you go," Sunday said. "Call Darcie and ask her to join us at high noon."

"I will," Mecana said. They got in their cars and drove away.

CHAPTER 5

A day and a half later, Mecana showed a border patrol trooper his old police badge and he and DeMax crossed the border.

Mecana asked DeMax to look under the seat. He reached under and pulled out a machine pistol.

"There are three clips in the glove box," Mecana said. "You know how to use it."

"Simple enough," DeMax said. He got the clips and stuck one in the pistol. "Why didn't you use this when we were chasing Candy Kane?"

"I just put it there for that reason," Mecana said.

"Maybe it will save our ass," DeMax said.

"It's not only the bad guys we have to worry about. If the police show up we might be in trouble with them, too," Mecana said. He took his Glock out of his shoulder holster, checked it, and put it back. "There's a cantina up the road.

I'm hungry, let's get some tacos. I think better when I'm not hungry."

"You got any pesos?" DeMax asked.

"Nah, they'll take American money," Mecana said and drove up to the curb and cut the engine off. DeMax stuck the pistol back under the seat and they both got out and walked up to the taco stand.

Mecana pointed at the menu, raised four fingers and mimed a drinking motion then handed the guy a twenty. A few minutes later the man handed back eight tacos, two bottles of water and no change.

"Didn't you mean four tacos," DeMax said.

"Yeah, but what the hell," he said and climbed back in the truck.

"Eat your tacos," Mecana said. "I got to piss first."

"Where? They don't have a restroom," DeMax said.

"I don't know, I'll find a place." Mecana opened the door and walked around the corner of the taco stand behind a tree and unzipped his pants. He heard a hammer click and felt a pistol hard against the back of his head.

"Your money, señor-" a voice began, but in the next instant, the man fell against him and the forty-five to the ground beside his leg. He turned around and DeMax was standing over a scrawny man on the ground out cold. His hair was combed and waxed into a peak over his head, wearing a dirty Hawaiian shirt and khaki pants. One of his flip flops had fallen off his foot. DeMax picked up his forty-five.

"Didn't take you long to get in trouble," DeMax said.

"I was concentrating on peeing," Mecana said and zipped up his pants.

"Could have been your last time," DeMax said.

"Yeah," Mecana said.

"Guy's waking up," DeMax grabbed the hombre on the ground by the pants and picked him up.

"Hang on to him and put him in the truck," Mecana said.

DeMax held his belt and pushed the man into the truck. He was trying to focus his eyes. He blinked, blinked again, and stared at DeMax in a daze in front of the open truck door.

"Let me go," he said. Mecana got in the driver side and DeMax stuck the forty-five in his belt, pushed the man in the truck and closed the door.

"What's your name, amigo?" Mecana asked.

"El Gallo," he said.

"What's that mean?"

"The Rooster," he said.

"You got any hens?" DeMax said.

"When I want one," he said.

"You're not much bigger than a rooster. You know anything about a guy from Texas named Douglas Bradford being found dead in an alley here recently?"

"I heard about it."

"You know who did it?" Mecana said.

"Don't know. Let me go," Rooster said.

"You do anything besides rob people?" Mecana said.

"None of your business," Rooster said.

"I don't think you understand your predicament Rooster," Mecana said. "I can kill you in self-defense for trying to rob me."

"Not here," Rooster said.

"I won't ask anybody," Mecana said.

"You want to kill him or should I," DeMax said and stuck Rooster's .45 against his head.

"Rooster, you know who murdered Douglas. Tell me and we won't kill you," Mecana said.

DeMax cocked the hammer. "Just say when."

"Anytime you want," Mecana said.

Rooster rolled his eyes back and forth between DeMax and Mecana, his breathing labored. "Chavez," he finally said. "Bad hombre. Let me go now."

"You see him do it," Mecana said.

"No, heard about it,' Rooster said.

"He the one who's got the car and the girl?" Mecana said.

"Don't know," Rooster said. "Maybe the car, he has a wrecker service."

"Well isn't that convenient," Mecana said.

"Everybody knows, even police," Rooster said.

"Where is he?" Mecana said.

"I tell you and I'll get out?" Rooster said.

"No. Show me," he said and pulled back out on the street.

Rooster pointed to the front. "Go to Roselle Street and turn left."

Mecana turned left and drove down the street. There was somebody selling something every few feet on both sides of the street. Some running out to the truck when traffic slowed down.

"There," Rooster said. "That big building on the left. If they see me they'll kill me for bringing you here."

"They know you?" Mecana asked.

"Yes."

"Then you're one of them," DeMax said.

"No. Everybody knows them."

"What do you do besides rob people?" Mecana said.

"A tourist guide," Rooster said.

"You got to be kidding," DeMax said.

"No, I speak good English and show people around."

"And rob them," Mecana said.

"Sometimes."

"You got family?" DeMax asked.

"Alfaro, mi tío, my mama's brother. She's dead now. Don't know who my papa is."

"I've heard enough," Mecana said and pulled over.

"Okay, tourist guide, what's that sign say on that shitty-looking building?" Mecana asked.

"Chavez Wrecker Service," Rooster said.

"They got the car," Mecana said. "Bet money on it."

"Don't know. Let me go," Rooster said.

"Hush," DeMax said.

A young tall man with long black hair walked out of the building and looked at the truck. He could see the Texas plates. He fished his phone out of his pocket and a few minutes later another man walked out of the building. He was older, shorter, wearing a black Stetson, a blue western shirt, and jeans with a big brass belt buckle and cowboy boots. He had his phone in his hand. The young one took a pistol from his back and let it down to the side of his leg and they started walking toward the truck. Three more men came out of the building and stopped in front of the truck.

"Rooster, get out," Mecana said.

"No, I stay with you. They'll kill me for sure," he said. "We leave now."

"They can outgun us," DeMax said. "I think he's right."

"Yeah, we'll have to have a better plan when we come back," Mecana said.

"Go home," Rooster said.

"Can't do that but a retreat is in order now." Mecana started the truck, threw it in reverse, turned the wheels and spun around. He floor-boarded it and hauled ass.

A van ran out in front of the truck, blocking it, as a jeep sped up behind them.

"Oh shit," Mecana said and stopped.

While Mecana and DeMax were watching the Mexicans, Rooster jumped out of the truck and took off running. Two of the men in the jeep opened fire with machine guns and Rooster hit the ground and crawled behind a parked car. Mecana and DeMax followed him out the same door and dove over a road barrier into a ditch, bullets flying all around them and peppering Mecana's new truck.

Rooster scooted over to the door of a shop and ran inside and out the back door. Mecana and DeMax jumped up and followed Rooster with their weapons in their hands. Rooster motioned them down an alley, ran through an old dilapidated building and out the other side.

He stopped and looked back but there was no one there. He lifted a manhole cover and dropped down into the sewer. Mecana and DeMax did the same and slid the cover back over the hole. They heard voices rattling in Spanish and two of them stepped on the manhole cover as they ran by. After about thirty minutes, Rooster raised the manhole cover slightly and peeked out both ways. No one was there. He slid the manhole cover off the hole. "Follow me," he said and climbed out.

"Where you goin'?" DeMax said.

"They'll be back. Come with me," Rooster said as they climbed out. He slid the cover back over the hole. "I have a place we can go, hurry." He broke into a run and Mecana and Demax did the same to keep up.

"You're not taking us back to them, are you?" Mecana said.

"No," Rooster said. "Sorry I tried to rob you."

"You wouldn't be if you had got my money," Mecana said. "You're just saying that because you need us now."

"Helping you too," he said.

"You are," Mecana agreed.

"Come on, let's go," Rooster said and took off running again.

"Damn, I just lost another truck," Mecana said in pursuit of Rooster.

"We could have lost our ass," DeMax said running along side Mecana.

"True, I'll claim it was stolen and buy another one."

"Come on," Rooster said, looking back over his shoulder as he slowed down.

Mecana and DeMax caught up and followed Rooster through a maze of people on the streets as the evening sun was disappearing on the horizon. They ran down a rock road several hundred yards and came to a six-foot chain link fence surrounding an electric tower. Rooster walked up to the gate, stuck his hand in his pocket and came out with a key and unlocked a padlock. They went in and Rooster reached through the gate and re-locked it.

"Man, we could get fried in here," DeMax said.

"We'll be alright now," Rooster said.

They made their way to a small wooden building with no windows, sitting in the corner of the compound.

"Come in," Rooster said and when they went in Rooster turned on a light. There were beds, a water bowl, a small refrigerator and a two-burner hot plate.

"Anyone else know about this?" DeMax said.

"No one except mi tío Alfaro. He works here," Rooster said.

"What's he do?" Mecana said.

"Checks the power output," Rooster said.

"They don't have anyone at night?" Mecana said.

"Police patrol comes by every once in a while, but the gate's locked, they don't have a key."

"What the hell good does it do for them to come by then?" DeMax said.

"They see anyone in here they'll shoot them."

"Now you tell us," Mecana said.

"Find a place to sleep and I'll turn off the light," Rooster said. "We'll borrow Alfaro's car in the morning and head for the border. His boy will pick him up here when he gets off. If you have to go to the baño watch out for headlights. We rest now."

"I'll call Darcie and let her know we're okay," Mecana said and started dialing. "Don't think I'll tell her about the truck just yet."

CHAPTER 6

Darcie called Sunday after speaking to Mecana.

"Mecana said he hasn't found Angela yet and that he and DeMax are hiding from the guys who have the car. I'm going to Mexico."

"I'll call Simon and go with you," Sunday said.

"Nothing you can do as a cop," Darcie said.

"No, but I can help you. I don't want anything to happen to them," Sunday said. "It would be my fault."

"Okay, we'll catch a flight to El Paso and rent a car. Mecana would just tell me to stay here if he knew I was coming so I'm not calling him until we get there."

"I'll meet you at the airport," Sunday said.

Darcie booked a redeye for 12:25 a.m. Four hours later, they touched down in El Paso. After renting a car, Darcie called Mecana.

"I told you not to come," Mecana said.

"That's why I didn't call you before I got here," Darcie said, "Sunday came with me. Where can I find you?"

"Wait a minute." Mecana took the phone from his ear. "Rooster, turn the light on." Rooster crawled over to the wall and flipped on the light switch.

"My wife's at the airport, where's a place she can meet us?"

"We'll meet her at the border at 8 a.m. Gate 15."

Mecana put the phone back to his ear. "Hang out at the airport and meet us at 8 a.m. at border gate 15."

"We'll be there, Sherlock," Darcie said.

Mecana repeated "8 a.m., gate 15."

"Got it. Oh, and I rented a black Honda van," Darcie said. "Don't be mad. You know you need me."

"I can never be mad at you for too long. I always need you."

"See you in the morning," she said.

"Goodbye," Mecana said and stuck the phone back in his pocket.

"Darcie's coming here?" DeMax asked.

"Yeah, and bringing Sunday with her."

"Not good," DeMax said.

"I don't know, they're tough," Mecana said.

"So are the hombres we're facing," DeMax said. "Might be best to call this off. I think Angela's dead anyway."

"Maybe, but I have to make sure," Mecana said.

"Go home," Rooster said. "They will kill you. Too many to fight."

"He's right," DeMax said.

"You can go home if you want to, DeMax ," Mecana said. "You don't owe me any favors."

"Not leaving unless you do, and I don't think you are. Let's get on with it."

"Rooster, if they kept her alive where would they take her?" Mecana asked.

"May not," Rooster said.

"Let's say they did?"

"Sell her in the sex slave market," Rooster said.

"Where?" Mecana asked.

"Many places, even in other countries," Rooster said. "She young and pretty?"

"Yes," Mecana said.

"Might keep her a while before selling her."

"Who? Chavez?"

"Yes, and pass her around as a reward to his men."

"Where would she be?" DeMax said.

"Maybe at Palamar."

"What's that?"

"Juan Chavez's ranchero."

"Was that Chavez who came out of the building dressed like a cowboy?" Mecana asked.

"Yes, he dresses like that all the time," Rooster said.

"He the main man?

"She's probably dead. You'll die for nothing."

"Did you have anything to do with it?" Mecana said.

"No," Rooster said.

"You think Darcie and Sunday should be here for this?" De Max said.

"No, but they are," Mecana said.

"Police on Chavez's side. No way you win," Rooster said. "Rest now." Rooster turned off the light.

The next morning, a 1988 Chevrolet Caprice was stirring up dust, headed toward the compound.

Mecana peeked out the door and saw the car. "That your uncle?"

Rooster peeked out. "Yes, that's Alfaro. We go as soon a he gets here." He opened the door and they walked out.

"It's got Texas plates on it," Mecana said. "He must have stole it."

"Borrowed it," Rooster said.

"From who?" DeMax said.

"He don't know," Rooster said.

Mecana and DeMax couldn't help but grin.

Alfaro unlocked the gate, walked up to Rooster and handed him the keys and walked away as if Mecana and DeMax weren't there.

"Get in," Rooster said. Mecana got up front and DeMax in the back and they headed for the border.

Rooster pulled into a parking spot next to a market facing the check points and they waited for Darcie to drive through. At three minutes to 8 she drove up to gate fifteen and the guard waved her through.

"That's her, pull out in the road so she can see me," Mecana said. Rooster drove out in front of the van and stopped.

"We should get away from here," Rooster said. "Bad place to be."

"Okay, I'll get in with her and follow you," Mecana said.

Rooster nodded and waited for Mecana to get out and drove away.

Mecana jumped in the van. "Hi babe, follow that Caprice."

Darcie accelerated to get behind it. "Where are we going?"

"I don't know but don't lose him," Mecana said, leaned over and kissed Darcie on the cheek.

"Glad I'm here," Darcie said.

"Me too," Mecana said and turned to the back. "Thanks for coming, Sunday. We still don't know what happened to Angela yet. It's not looking good. Slim possibility she's still alive."

"That's what I was afraid of," Sunday said.

Rooster slowed down and turned off onto a dirt road with Darcie close behind.

After running down the road for a mile or two, he stopped under a tree and got out with DeMax. Darcie stopped next to his car and she, Sunday and Mecana got out.

"This is Rooster, ladies. Saved our ass when we ran into who I think are the ones who have Angela. Rooster, this is my wife Darcie," Mecana said, placing his hand on Darcie's shoulder, "and our lifelong friend Sunday."

"Buenos días señoritas," Rooster said.

"What're we doing here?" Mecana asked.

"This road winds through the brush to the border, and we can drive right on into the US."

"Done it before, haven't you," Mecana said.

"Many times, but I'm not coming back this time. Here's your map. Everything I remember about Palamar. I'm going home now." He turned around and opened the Caprice.

Mecana pushed him back from the door and closed it. "Not yet," he said. Rooster walked around to the other side of the car and leaned against the fender, staring off into space and sulking.

"Why does he want to be a rooster," Sunday asked.

"Maybe he thinks he is one," DeMax said.

"He looks like one with that hair," Sunday said.

"He's a few bricks short of a load," DeMax said.

"We've got more important things to do than analyze Rooster," Mecana said. "Tonight, DeMax and I will see if we can get a look at the car at the wrecker service. Might tell us something we need to know."

"Before you head out we'll go get something to eat," Darcie said. "Nobody knows me and Sunday."

"Make sure no one follows you two coming back."

Darcie and Sunday got in the van and took off.

"Anyone at the wrecker place late at night, Rooster?" Mecana asked.

"Someone's there all the time."

"How many," DeMax said.

"Don't know," Rooster said. "How ever many it takes to kill you."

"They have a skylight?" Mecana said.

"Yes, I think so," Rooster said.

"You think or you know?" Mecana said.

"They do."

"If you know what happened to Angela, tell us now before it's too late."

"I don't know," Rooster said. "I swear."

CHAPTER 7

Darcie and Sunday returned and they all ate tacos and drank warm Cokes.

"Rooster, do they make anything besides tacos around here?" DeMax said.

"Anything you want," Rooster said.

"We were trying to be quick," Darcie said.

"They're good," DeMax said. "Not complaining. How're we going to get on the roof, Mecana?"

"They may have a fire escape ladder. If not, I don't know 'til I look at it. May have to go in on the ground."

"You think seeing the car is necessary?" Darcie said.

"Yes, it may tell us what they wanted the car for and if Angela is alive," Mecana said.

"If there's bullet holes in both seats she's not," Sunday said.

"I would think that too," Mecana said. "Everybody find you a resting place, we're going to need it. DeMax, stand guard for a while."

"Did I volunteer?" DeMax said.

"Yep," Mecana said and stretched out beside Darcie in the van. By the time he was comfortable, Sunday turned around in the van seat.

"Mecana, Doug Bradford never represented Big Dog, but he got Biggen off for burglary three months ago."

"What!" Mecana said and sat up. "If he knew Biggen then Big Dog knew him. Angela may not have known what was going on but Bradford did and Angela was caught in the crossfire."

"I hope she's alive and wasn't part of it," Sunday said.

"You're all loco," Rooster said.

"That might include you, too, Rooster," DeMax said.

"There's more," Sunday said. "Juan Chavez was born in Mexico, served five years for drug dealing and deported back to Mexico. Later tried for murder and got off. Wanted for murder and smuggling now.

"I think we're connecting some of the dots now," Mecana said. "Bradford must have been set up for a hit. He has something to do with all this besides being an attorney for a bad guy. You know why they wanted to kill him, Rooster?"

"No," he said.

"You wouldn't lie to us, would you, Rooster," DeMax said.

Rooster shook his head no.

"You do and I'll make you a hen," DeMax said.

"Chavez will come after you," Rooster said.

"Won't have to, we're going after him," Mecana said. "Girls, you stay here and keep an eye on Rooster in the van. We'll borrow his car and DeMax and I will check out the building later tonight. Give us about three hours after we leave. If we're not back by then, call me. If no answer, head for the border and go home."

"I'll decide that, Sherlock," Darcie said.

"Was afraid of that," Mecana said.

"You don't come back, I'll come after you," Darcie said.

"I'll be with her," Sunday said.

"Don't worry, I'll be back," Mecana said.

"You better be," Darcie said.

"Give me the keys to your car, Rooster," Mecana said.

Rooster dropped the keys into his hand. "Bring it back, it's not mine."

"It's not your uncle's either."

The distant sound of an engine roaring suddenly grabbed everyone's attention.

"Someone's coming hell-bent for leather. Everyone get in the van, I'll drive," Mecana said.

"I can't leave Alfaro's car."

"Get in the van before I throw you in," DeMax said.

"You tell anyone you were coming here, Rooster?" Mecana said.

"Only Alfaro," he said.

"Well someone must have gotten to your uncle, willingly or unwillingly," Mecana said.

"If they did he's dead now," Rooster said.

A truck appeared speeding down the dirt road with two in the cab and three men in the back carrying automatic weapons.

"You were right, Rooster," DeMax said. "It's Chavez."

"We're getting out of here," Mecana said and opened the van door. "Get in and hang on."

DeMax picked up his machine pistol and got in the van. Darcie and Sunday pulled out their guns and jumped in. Rooster sunk down to the floor of the van and curled up like a cat.

Mecana stomped the gas pedal to the floor and the van peeled out, throwing up dirt.

A thick cloud of dust rose up from the speeding vehicles as they approached each other. The truck spun around, headlights cutting through the dust, and picked up the back of the van as it weaved down the dirt road. The dust bellowed out and streaks of gunfire hit the van in several places, busting out a rear window and sinking into the backseat foam, inches short of DeMax and Sunday. Rooster was curled up in a tighter ball on the floorboard.

"Stay down," Mecana yelled. They reached the highway and Mecana darted in front of a car to block their view, pieces of glass still falling from the busted back window of the van.

The truck was catching up, bullets whizzing by without regard for innocent people on the highway. A police car showed up behind the truck. The men in the back of the truck turned their fire on the police car. The windshield busted out and the police car came to an abrupt stop in the middle of the road and caught fire. Cars were turning off the highway wherever they could from both directions, leaving the van and truck as the only ones on the highway.

Mecana used his Marine voice to yell at everyone. "I'm going to turn off behind that building on the right. Get out and follow me as soon as I stop," he said. Everyone nodded except Rooster under the seat.

Mecana left the highway and ran the van behind a big brick two-story building and stopped. "Let's go," he said.

They all piled out except Rooster. Mecana stood at the open van door looking at him curled up underneath the seat. "Come on, Rooster, get out."

"No. Staying here."
"They'll kill you, come on, damn it."
"No," he repeated.
"I can't wait," Mecana said and ran to the others and motioned for them to follow. He ran around the corner of the building to the front as the truck disappeared behind the back. He raised his hand and made a shooting motion with his hand and they continued around the building. He peeked around the corner – all of the men were out of the truck approaching the van, firing at it with Rooster still inside. People were running out of the building in all directions in a foot race to get away.

Mecana motioned again, pointing his finger at the truck. Everyone nodded and readied their weapons. "Now," he yelled and they stepped out from the corner, dropping two of the men instantly in a barrage of fire and ducked back behind the wall. A man left standing turned running at them, firing. Chavez and his driver got back in the truck. Mecana and everyone ran to the other side of the building and stopped around the corner. They heard the truck engine.

The man chasing them flew around the corner and DeMax blasted him before he knew what was happening. Mecana ran back to the other corner. The truck came into view. The driver stopped and Chavez and the driver jumped out of the truck firing at him and he hit the ground. Darcie, Sunday and DeMax all showed up from behind Chavez and the driver from the other side of the building. Chavez jerked the driver in front of him and they shot the driver. Chavez's black cowboy hat blew off. He held the dead driver up then pulled him down with him as he hit the ground. The sound of screaming sirens was not far away.

"We're in a pickle again," Darcie said.

DeMax ran to Chavez, pushed the dead driver off him, kicked him in the face and grabbed the gun out of his hands.

"Everybody get in the truck," Mecana said. "The van's done for. DeMax, give me his phone." DeMax rammed his hand in Chavez's pocket and pitched the phone to Mecana.

"Soon as the police check the van they'll know who they're looking for," Darcie said.

"Probably do already," Mecana said. "DeMax, bring Chavez."

DeMax threw Chavez over his shoulder and dropped him in the bed of the truck, unconscious, and climbed in beside him. "Guess Rooster's dead," DeMax said.

"Would have to be," Mecana said behind the wheel, looking over at the bullet-ridden van. "He wouldn't come with me."

Just then, Rooster's head bobbed up from inside the van like a cork and went down again.

"You see that, Mecana," Sunday said.

"What?"

"Rooster's alive, I just saw him in the van," Sunday said.

"I think I did too," Darcie said.

"Can't be," Mecana said.

Rooster staggered out of the van holding his left shoulder, a trickle of blood running down his arm and a bullet hole through his waxed rooster peak hair.

Darcie and Sunday ran to him and helped him back to the truck, squeezing him into the cab.

"My uncle is going to kill me for losing his car," Rooster said.

Darcie and Sunday looked at each other and shook their heads. Sunday pulled a scarf out of her pocket and wrapped it around Rooster's arm. "He's just nicked," she said.

"You've got to be the luckiest man alive," Darcie said.

"For now anyway," Mecana said. "Let's get the hell out of here."

Mecana wheeled the truck out in the road and headed down the highway. Four police cars came by going the other way.

"They think we're still there," Sunday said.

"Not for long," Rooster said. "You see that side street turning off to the left? Take it, it goes to an old empty building."

"On my way, little man," Mecana said.

Mecana made a turn on the side road and ran up and over a hill.

"There's the building, park the truck inside," Rooster said.

Mecana whipped the truck inside and came to a stop.

"Everybody out, have a look," Mecana said.

They all got out of the truck. DeMax carried Chavez on his shoulder to a corner and dropped him on the floor. He moaned and opened his eyes. DeMax pulled Chavez's belt off, tied his hands behind his back and sat him up against the wall. Blood was splattered across his face from DeMax's shoe. "Rooster, come here," DeMax said.

"What you want?" Rooster said.

"May need you if he don't speak English," DeMax said.

"He does," Rooster said.

Chavez recognized Rooster. "El Gallo," Chavez said and started speaking to Rooster in Spanish.

"What'd he say?" Mecana asked.

"He said he's going to cut off my —" Rooster began but trailed off, looking at Darcie and Sunday. "He said he's going to kill me."

"It's Chavez who needs to worry about that if he doesn't tell me what happened to Angela," Mecana said and squatted down in front of Chavez. "What happened to the woman who was with the man you killed?"

Chavez stared at Mecana and didn't answer.

"Rooster says you understand English." Mecana reached down and drew a 10-inch knife from a scabbard strapped to the inside of his leg. "You think I was shittin' you? DeMax, pull his pants off."

"I didn't know you had that," DeMax said.

"Added it to my arsenal after what we went through with Candy," Mecana said.

"Grab a boot, Rooster," DeMax said. "I'll get the other one."

DeMax and Rooster each picked up a leg, got a grip on a boot and pulled them off. Then Demax yanked the pants off Chavez. He was wearing black silk shorts.

"Ladies, why don't you stand guard over there," Mecana said, pointing to the entrance. "This may get nauseating."

Chavez kept wiping his bloody face on his cowboy shirt as he talked. "No," he said. "Not me. I business man."

"He's lying," Rooster said. "Earlier he was bragging about killing the gringo because he double-crossed the cartel. Never say what he did with the girl. I didn't tell you earlier because he would have killed me, too."

"We're going to find out one way or another," Mecana said.

"You kill my uncle?" Rooster said.

"He try to kill me," Chavez said.

"So you did kill him."

"Sí," Chavez said and spit on Rooster.

Rooster slapped him across the face several times before DeMax pulled him off.

"Back off, Rooster, we'll take care of him," DeMax said.

"Give me a gun," Rooster said.

"No," Mecana said. "Where is she, Chavez?"

"She dead with the double-crossing gringo," Chavez said.

"What did you do with the body," Mecana said.

"Throw it away," Chavez said.

Sunday ran over to Chavez. "Is this her?" She showed him a picture of Angela.

"Sí," Chavez said.

Sunday raised her gun to Chavez's head.

"No, no, I lie. She alive at my ranchero," Chavez said.

Sunday lowered the gun and stared at Chavez.

Mecana reached over to Sunday and placed the barrel of her gun back to Chavez's forehead. "If you don't take us to the girl she'll blow your brains out. After I castrate you for the fun of it and send a picture to your men."

Chavez's eyes were glued to Mecana's knife as he rolled it around in his hand.

Mecana stuck his knife against Chavez's silk shorts and his heart began to pound fast enough to see under the purple cowboy shirt.

"No, wait, I go. You get girl, you let me go. Deal?" Chavez said.

"If anyone fires one shot at us we'll kill you," Mecana said.

"Put his pants on," Darcie said. "Can't stand to look at him anymore."

Rooster and DeMax stood him up and made him step into his jeans.

"Boots," Chavez said.

Sunday reached down and threw one of Chavez's fancy boots out an open window, followed by the other one. "You won't need them if Angela's dead, you will be too."

Sunday's phone rang. "It's Simon," she said and answered. "We don't know yet. We may soon. I'll call you as soon as we know." She dropped the phone to her side. "He hung up. He was crying."

"Let's go find out," Mecana said. "Get in the cab, asshole. Rooster, get in the back with DeMax. No gun, he'll cover you."

"Before you try to protect us, forget it," Darcie said. "We're going with you."

"You better believe it," Sunday said.

CHAPTER 8

Mecana pulled the truck over a couple of miles down the road. "There's a grocery store with a restroom. I'll stay with Chavez. DeMax, go keep an eye on Rooster and the girls. Someone's going to recognize this truck if we hang around here for very long. Bring me a big orange and a package of peanut butter crackers. Oh, and some duct tape if they have it, for Chavez."

"I'm afraid to let you go pee by your self," DeMax said and grinned.

"Get," Mecana said.

"What happened?" Darcie said.

"Nothing, go."

Darcie slid off the seat to the ground and looked back at Mecana. "I'll make you tell me later," she said and gave him a sly grin.

"Chavez, I don't really give a damn what happens to you but if we get Angela out alive I'll let you go. Whatever else you've done is somebody else's problem. You got me?"

"Sí señor," Chavez said.

"I hope to hell you do," Mecana said. "Lay down in the seat and keep your mouth shut."

Ten minutes later everyone was back. Darcie and Sunday got in. "Here's your orange and crackers, didn't have the tape," Darcie said.

"Rooster, you said this was the road to Chavez's place, right?"

"Yeah, four miles ahead, but I don't want to go."

"Fine with me but I'll keep the keys. We may need the car later."

"If I can't have the car might as well go with you and kill Chavez when I get the chance."

"Suit yourself. Get in." DeMax and Rooster climbed in the bed of the truck. "Let's go," Mecana said.

"DeMax told me what happened," Darcie said. "Want me to go with you to pee?"

"I'll wait," he said, giving Darcie a sideways look. He started the truck engine and took off out into the bare land with no trees or buildings.

"I can see why he's out here," Mecana said. "You can see for miles."

"Yeah, they probably already know we're coming," Darcie said.

"When we get there, you and Sunday stay in the truck," Mecana said. "I'm going to show Chavez. If they shoot me, haul ass before they kill you too. Won't do me any good for you to die. That goes for you too, Sunday. I'll bring him down with me."

"They'll have to kill me too," Darcie said.

"I think that goes for all of us," Sunday said.

Mecana shook his head. "Wasted breath."

On the other side of the next hill Chavez's ranchero came into view – a large two-story tiled-roof mansion with a tall rock fence and guards walking a catwalk behind the fence, heads sticking up over it.

Mecana drove a little closer and stopped the truck. "We'll wait here," he said.

"You think he's important enough for them not to kill you on sight," Darcie said.

"I big man. They do what I say," Chavez said.

"You better tell them to bring Angela to us." Mecana opened the door and got out, pulling Chavez with him, and left the engine running. "Rooster, if you want to get even with Chavez help us now. I'm going to give him his phone to tell them to bring her to us. Let me know what he's saying."

"He lies all the time," Rooster said. "Can I kill him if she don't come out?"

"Sure, why not," Mecana said. "Here's your phone, Chavez. Make the call, you said we had a deal."

"You wait and see, Rooster lie too," Chavez said.

"Call them," Mecana repeated.

Rooster moved closer to Chavez. "Turn the speaker on," he said. Chavez punched the speaker button and starting speaking Spanish.

A few moments later, Chavez stopped talking and handed the phone back to Mecana.

"What did he say?" Mecana asked.

"He said 'Bring her out quick I'm being held captive' but he didn't say what she looked like or if she was alive," Rooster said.

"She alive," Chavez said.

"That doesn't sound quite right," Mecana said and pushed Chavez back in the truck. "I didn't come all this way to leave without her. Here's the phone again, Chavez, now tell them to bring her to us or I'll throw your dead body out this truck."

"We make swap," Chavez said.

"I can go for that. Tell them."

Chavez dialed again and spoke quickly in Spanish.

"He do what I said?" Mecana asked Rooster.

"Yes," he said. The gate opened and two men came out carrying someone on a stretcher, walking toward the truck.

"I've got to go to her," Sunday said. Darcie got out of the truck and stood behind the open door.

"Wait, Sunday, let them get closer," Mecana said and grabbed her by the arm. "DeMax, when they get here put her in the back."

The two men carrying the stretcher walked up beside the truck carrying a woman. She wasn't moving. Sunday ran to her. "It's Angela," she said.

Chavez turned and kicked Darcie with both feet and jumped out of the seat. He tried to run but his hands were tied behind him.

The two men dropped the stretcher and took off running. DeMax picked Angela off the stretcher and put her in the truck bed, Sunday jumping in with her. Rooster grabbed the gun off of DeMax's shoulder and let loose on Chavez. He staggered a few feet forward and fell dead, face down. His men ran past him and Rooster killed them before they could reach the gate.

Darcie got in the truck and DeMax in the back. Mecana slid behind the wheel.

Two trucks came through the open gate carrying men with automatic weapons.

"Come on, Rooster," Mecana said. "Let's go."

"No, go ahead. I'll get them."

The two trucks were almost on them. Rooster blasted the windshields out, killing the drivers of the trucks which came to a sudden stop when they collided into each other. Several men hit the ground from the back of the trucks, firing at Rooster. Their bullets ripped him apart.

"Oh no, little guy, damn it!" Mecana said and spun the truck around. Chavez's men were taking the dead drivers out of the trucks.

Mecana glanced into the rearview mirror as they were speeding away and saw Rooster and Chavez lying on the ground dead, and Darcie looking at him through the back glass. Sunday was shaking her head, tears rolling down her cheeks.

"Angela is dead," Darcie said.

Mecana nodded and drove on in silence.

A few minutes later, Darcie spotted the trucks again. "They're gaining on us."

"Have to get to Rooster's trail to the border and get his car, we're almost out of gas."

Mecana dodged cars and trucks and turned onto the cutoff road, trucks in his rearview mirror. They turned onto the dirt road behind him. He let off the gas then accelerated and stirred up lots of dust between them and the trucks. He pulled up beside the Caprice. "Everybody in the car."

DeMax and Mecana were removing Angela from the truck. Sunday got in the Caprice and said, "Give her to me."

They sat the dead woman on Sunday's lap. Her face was severely bruised and her left arm twisted out of her shoulder socket. The only thing she had on were her panties and an unbuttoned red blouse. It was clear she had only been dead an hour or so.

Darcie got in the front of the car, DeMax and Sunday were in the back with the dead Angela.

Mecana fished the keys out of his pocket and stuck them in the ignition. "Hope this thing starts." He turned the key and it fired up. He jerked it into gear and took off down the dirt road. Washtub-size holes in the road made the car bounce up and down like a pogo stick. They came to a big overhanging tree limb. "Oh shit," Mecana said. "Have to go under it." The car cleared the limb by no more than a few inches. Thick brush dotted both sides of the dirt road.

"They can't get a truck under that," DeMax said.

In another two or thee miles they came to a fallen border fence and crossed into the USA.

"We're here," Mecana said. Two border patrol SUVs were coming towards them. The trucks had disappeared.

Mecana stopped the Caprice and cut the engine off. "Leave your weapons in the car and get out," he said.

They opened the doors, letting the foul smell of death out, and kept their hands up waiting for the border patrol.

"Thanks Rooster," Darcie said, looking back at the car and Mexico. "We won't forget you."

"Yeah, we wouldn't have made it without him," Mecana said.

"He was more of a man than I thought," DeMax said.

"We wouldn't have gotten Angela back without him," Sunday said. "Now I've got to make the hardest call I've ever made."

CHAPTER 9

Angela's family gathered around her grave to say their goodbyes. Simon looked like he had aged ten years in the last week, and his wife clung to him every step of the way to keep from going down.

Robert and Valisa were trying to comfort them but there was nothing anyone could say that would help. A parent never expects to lose a child before they go. It's the hardest thing these parents would ever endure in their life.

Simon and his wife walked over to Mecana and Darcie. "Thank you," Simon said, "for bringing my daughter back. It would've been even harder not knowing what happened to her."

"I'm just sorry we couldn't bring her back alive," Mecana said.

"Sunday warned me," Simon said, "but I wouldn't believe it. It's partly my fault for not checking Bradford out more before they became engaged. She was so happy."

"It's not your fault," Darcie said, hugging him.

"Thank you," his wife said. "We have to go now."

"Yes ma'am," Mecana said.

Sunday walked over to Mecana and Darcie, DeMax following. "It's such a shame," she said. "We came so close but couldn't get there soon enough."

"That will always stay with us," Darcie said.

"Always," Sunday agreed. "I'll keep you posted on what's happening. Haven't found anything that makes me think Angela knew what her boyfriend was up to. I'm going to keep after it until I know the whole story. It's good to know Chavez paid for what he did, but there's others to find before this can be put to rest. Going to start with Big Dog."

"If you need us again let me know," Mecana said.

"I will," Sunday said.

"I feel so sorry for Angela and her family," Darcie said.

"That's why I'm going to find out who was behind Bradford's set up and if Angela was innocent in all this. May not be something we want to know now. I mean, what if she wasn't?"

CHAPTER 10

Two days after the funeral, Mecana was sitting at his office desk watching a painter switch the name on the glass door from Mecana & Connors to Connors & Mecana.

He started thinking about Darcie and his upcoming trip to Austin to see the kids and confront Amanda's new boyfriend. He was supposed to be a rich businessman that wanted her and the kids to move into his mansion, sell their house and let him put the money into the stock market for them. The kids didn't want any part of it. Another dilemma he would have to deal with.

"It's done," the painter said, bringing Mecana out of his daydream. "Total is five hundred."

"For just switching the names?"

"Yep."

Mecana wrote a check handed it to him. He stuck it in his white overalls pocket, picked up his paint and brushes and closed the door on his way out.

Mecana's phone rang. It was Verves.

"How you doing, Chief," Mecana said.

"Been having some problems with my ticker. They got me wired up like a hot rod in my bed. Need to talk to you before Valisa comes back in here."

"What is it?" Mecana said.

"Sunday just left, said she was going to do some research on Chavez to find out who he worked for and go after them. I'm worried about her."

"Why is that?" Mecana said.

"She's determined to solve Angela's case. She doesn't know Chavez goes all the way back to when I found her as a baby and we took him to trial for murder. I was afraid to tell her. We never found the other guy with Chavez that night. Chavez got off on a technicality. If she digs that up she may find out things she would be better off not knowing."

"Like what?" Mecana asked.

"Like who her biological father is."

"Holy shit, you don't mean Chavez? That's hard to imagine."

"No, it wasn't Chavez. Read the file so you know what she's up against and keep an eye on her for me. No telling what could happen," Verves said. "I'll have Simon pull it for you."

"I'll take a look," Mecana said.

"Here comes Valisa. Thanks, bye," Verves said and hung up.

Mecana sat down behind the desk, looked at the newly-painted door and dialed Darcie.

"The door painted?" Darcie asked.

"Yeah, you owe me big time," Mecana said.

"We'll set up an installment plan," Darcie said and laughed.

"I like that," Mecana said. "I'll hold you to it. Got something I need to tell you. I got a call from the chief. He's in bad shape and wants us to keep an eye on Sunday for him. She may need us. I told him we would. I'll tell you about it when I get home to collect my payment. I think I'm going to cancel my trip to Austin. Probably better anyway for now. Amanda is breaking in a new boyfriend."

"Sunday is coming over this afternoon," Darcie said. "I thought you would be leaving for Austin."

"I'll call the kids and postpone the trip," Mecana said.

"If you want to come on home I'll make a payment on my account before Sunday gets here, but it better be soon."

"Might get a speeding ticket."

"You go too fast anyway," Darcie said.

"We'll see about that." Mecana dropped the phone in his pocket, stood up, pushed his chair back and headed out. He looked at the Connors & Mecana on the door one more time and switched off the lights.

"May turn out to be my ace in the hole," he thought to himself and grinned.

The next morning, Mecana made his way to police headquarters around 10:30 to pick up the file.

When he walked into Simon's office an old manila file folder was waiting on the desk, Simon behind it pouring a cup of coffee.

"Hey Mecana," Simon said. "There's the file Robert wanted you to look at. It went cold years ago and may have been a good thing for Sunday. I understand why he's concerned. I tried to take Sunday off the case but she threatened to quit if I did. That's why Robert called you."

"He told me what he was afraid off," Mecana said.

"I want to get to the bottom of this but I agree with Robert," Simon said. "I think it would be better for her not to take this trip down memory lane."

"The way I see it, I think it's her call," Mecana said. "I'm not going to take that away from her. But I'm not going to go out of my way to make sure she knows, either."

"Take a look at the file and you may want to rethink that."

"I know this has to be hard on you Simon."

"With a furious anger, I want any and everyone that had anything to do with Angela's murder to pay for it. But I would hope Sunday doesn't."

"I spent some time with her in Mexico," Mecana said. "She's tough. I think her biological father is just a name. Robert Verves is her real daddy in her heart. And I think it's even stronger now because of you and Angela."

"Whoever he is is not the problem. It's what happens if he is still alive." Simon picked up the file and handed it to Mecana. "Take a look."

"Where's Sunday," Mecana said, opening the folder.

"Already working on the case," Simon said. "Robert puts a lot of trust in you, remember that."

"I will," Mecana said.

CHAPTER 11

Sunday didn't go to the office. She stopped by her parent's house to check on her dad and headed for Shooters Pool Hall.

Turns out Big Dog was bailed out on a half-million-dollar cash retainer put up by the law firm Bradford worked at. And no one there was talking without a subpoena.

So she went to find Big Dog.

When she drove up to the pool hall she heard the sound of pool balls hitting each other and went inside. Four guys she didn't know were playing pool and drinking beer.

Biggen was sitting in a corner fondling a Mexican girl on his lap. He saw Sunday, pushed the girl off and stood up. The girl moved away from him and stood against the wall.

"Hey everybody, a lady cop just walked in," Biggen said. "Everybody grab your balls before she steals 'em."

"Where's Big Dog?"

"He ain't been here since he got out of jail. He knew you would be coming around."

"When you see him, tell him I'll cut him a deal for the right information," Sunday said.

"He ain't no stool pigeon, he knows the same thing would happen to him that happened to those white birds in Mexico," Biggen said.

"If there's anyone else here who knows why Doug Bradford and Angela Necessary were murdered there's a ten-thousand-dollar reward," Sunday said. "You can call any precinct with information. We won't reveal anyone's identity, either."

"Thanks, but no thanks," Biggen said, with the others nodding approval.

"What happened to Squirt," Sunday said.

"He met an unfortunate accident." Biggen and everyone else laughed except the girl.

"In your business, everybody's time runs out," Sunday said.

"Yours too," Biggen said.

The girl standing against the wall like a statue was trying to disappear.

"Young lady, I don't think you're old enough to be in here. Get out." The girl darted past Sunday and out the door. Everyone got quiet and stared at Sunday. She back stepped to the door and went outside to her car.

Sunday pulled away from the curb and stopped in the next block at a red light. The girl from Shooters ran out from a side street and pulled on the locked door handle, gibbering in a mix of English and Spanish. She had both hands on the window. Sunday could see there was nothing in them so she unlocked the door. The girl jumped in and fell to the floorboard.

"I don't speak much Spanish. What do you want?" Sunday said.

The girl raised her head up, looking surprised. "I know something about the murders."

"Stay there until I tell you to get up," Sunday said. The light changed and she kicked the horses watching the rear view mirror. Nothing unusual happened.

Sunday drove across town to her house and cut the engine off inside the garage. The girl started to get up.

"Wait until I make sure no one followed us," Sunday said. She drew her gun and waited for a few minutes. Nothing.

"Okay, let's go in. Stay close to me." They walked through the kitchen into the living room. Sunday closed the blinds and they sat down on the couch, Sunday still holding her gun. She laid it beside her and took a pen and pad out of her pocket. "Okay, I have to take some notes," she said.

"Will I get the reward?" the girl asked.

"Depends on what you know. What's your name?"

"Margarita Perez." Sunday wrote it on the note pad.

"How old are you," Sunday asked and continued taking notes.

"Sixteen," she said.

"Then you didn't belong in there. What do you know about the murders?"

"Biggen makes me do whatever he wants. He said he would kill my mother and little brother if I didn't."

"He may be just telling you that," Sunday said.

"No! I saw him shoot a man for not giving him money for a fix."

"You on any drugs?"

"Heroin."

"You pay for drugs the way I think you do?"

"Yes," Margarita said.

"Go on," Sunday said.

"I had to go with Biggen and Big Dog to meet with a group of Mexicans who didn't speak English. They were setting up a trip to Mexico for the lawyer and his girlfriend because he was skimming money from the cash he took to Mexico."

"You know anyone from this group?"

"No. They work for Chavez. He wanted the lawyer to think he was making his regular trip."

"Did the woman know why he was going to Mexico?"

"They say she thought they were going on a vacation, but they intended to sell her to a brothel."

"She didn't know any of that?"

"Don't think so."

"Did they say what her name was?"

"No."

"Did you know Chavez?" Sunday said.

"I know he will kill you if you don't do what he says."

"Chavez is dead. You don't have to be afraid of him anymore," Sunday said.

"Are you sure?" Margarita asked.

"Yes," Sunday said. "I was there when he was killed in Mexico. What else do you know?"

"A limo drove up when we were talking to the Mexicans and Big Dog walked over to it," Margarita said. "A man in the back opened the door but he didn't get out. Big Dog stood by the door talking to him. They were speaking in English. The man in the limo sounded American. Big Dog called him Mr. Money."

"Mr. Money? Did you see him?"

"He stayed in the car but I could see his hands. He was white and old."

"Anything else?"

"No. Will that get me the reward?"

"That's a step in the right direction," Sunday said. "I have to make a call to find a safe house for you and your family until we sort this out. You have an address?"

"In the basement at 4237 Riesman Street. It's about five blocks from the pool hall. You sure have a lot of questions."

"It's necessary," Sunday said.

"That reminds me," Margarita said. "Big Dog said he was going to kill necessary. I didn't know what he meant."

"I do," Sunday said. "If Mr. Money is the one we're after, you will have to be a witness before you can get the reward. If you do, it will come with a stipulation that you are put in a rehabilitation program."

"That's what I want. They will sell me to a brothel when Biggen gets tired of me," Margarita said. "How come someone like you doesn't speak Spanish?"

"It's a long story I don't have time for," Sunday said. "You've given me some very valuable information. I'll make sure you get credit for it."

"Now what?"

"We wait for the unit to pick you up," Sunday said.

"Will the cops protect me and my family?" Margarita asked.

"Yes, and they'll give you a new start somewhere when this is all over."

CHAPTER 12

Mecana and Darcie sat down on the couch and opened the file and started reading, passing pages from one to the other until they finished.

"What a horrible thing to happen to her," Darcie said. "She was lucky it was Robert and Simon who found her."

"Could have been a wasted life if she had been put through the system," Mecana said. "I think the woman who delivered her knew who her father was, but was too afraid to say."

"Yeah, that's what I was thinking," Darcie said. "He was probably involved with drugs, too."

"I can see now why Robert and Simon didn't want her to have to relive it."

"What do you think we should do now?"

"I don't know," Mecana said.

"You think her father is still alive?"

"Good question. I wonder if the midwife is still alive. We have her name, may be able to get his from her. Think I'll find out."

"Might be as simple as running a net check on her."

"We can start there."

"I'll see if I can find Juanita What's-her-face," Darcie said.

"Juanita Gonzales," Mecana said. "She said Sunday's mother Maria worked as a nanny for someone but wouldn't say who. Probably the married father. There should be documents in Maria's name for salary and other things. Even the place they were killed at. If we can find out who, maybe we can prevent the inevitable from happening to her. I think I'll call her and see what she's doing."

"It's her case, don't try and take it over," Darcie said.

"I won't."

Mecana called Sunday. "Hey kid," he said. "What are you doing?"

"I found a witness that knows what happened. Bradford was killed for skimming off money. My witness is a sixteen-year-old heroin addict but I think she's telling the truth. Even better, she remembered the name of a main man in the deal who's calling all the shots. They call him The Cleaner. I'm running a check on him now."

"Well you've had a hell of a day," Mecana said. "You need any help?"

"Not now, but I may if I have to go get the boss. I can't think of anyone I'd rather have with me than you two."

"That puts me in a position where I need to be better than I've ever been," Mecana said.

"You will be," Sunday said. "I'm waiting for a unit to pick up my witness. Her name is Margarita Perez. I'm running a check on her too. I'm at my house."

"How long you been there?" Mecana asked.

"About an hour."

"You should leave now. They figure things out pretty quickly. May be missing the girl already and are putting two and two together."

"Yeah, you're right. I'll head to police headquarters downtown."

"I'll meet you there," Mecana said.

Before Sunday could reply, the front door came crashing down with Big Dog and Biggen running in armed to the teeth. Sunday pointed her gun at them, put the phone on speaker, and dropped it behind her. Mecana could hear every word.

"Put your gun down," Big Dog said. "The boss wants you." Sunday dropped her gun.

Margarita broke to run to the kitchen door but Biggen put at least ten rounds in her body before she could take three steps. She wobbled against the wall and slid down to the floor, her head leaning against the baseboard, her big brown eyes in an open stare with blood running across the floor like a river.

"Figured that little tramp would turn me in," Biggen said.

"She was just sixteen, you bastard," Sunday said, staring at Margarita's dead eyes.

"She was a piece of shit," Big Dog said. "Tie the cop's hands, Biggen."

"I warned you not to come back, bitch," Biggen said.

Mecana cut the phone off. "You hear that," he asked Darcie.

"Yeah, let's go," she said.

They jumped in the truck and smoked the street as Mecana let the hammer down like a racecar.

"She's not that far from here if we don't catch a train at Smyth," Mecana said. "I'll cut across the pasture at Corinth."

There was gun fire. People in nearby houses were coming out to look, then ran back inside when they saw Sunday's front door knocked down.

"Get in the truck," Big Dog said. Biggen pushed Sunday out the door, her hands tied behind her back and her gun stuck inside his belt, to a black truck painted with gold skulls. Biggen opened a door and lifted her in.

"I might have a surprise for you before I kill you," Biggen said and ran his hand up between Sunday's legs.

"You'll have to kill me first, shithead."

Big Dog backed the truck out and roared down the street.

"Where are you taking me?" Sunday asked.

"Shut up," Big Dog said. "You're lucky the boss wants to see you or I would've already killed you."

Mecana and Darcie stopped and pulled out their guns and ran into the open doorway, Mecana going one way and Darcie another. She saw the girl she thought to be Margarita lying dead on the floor.

"Nobody else here," Mecana said. They ran back outside to get in the truck. A man was peeking out of the house next door. Mecana yelled at him. "You see which way they went? Detective Sunday is a friend of ours."

The man opened the door a little wider, stuck his arm out and pointed.

"Thanks," Mecana said. "What kind of car?"

"A big black truck with skulls on it," the man said.

"Ok. Call 911, there's a body in the house."

They got in the truck and took off in the direction the man had pointed.

"Darcie, will you call DeMax and tell him what the truck looks like. We're going to need him to join us in this chase."

Darcie dialed. "What you need, Darcie?" DeMax asked.

"Sunday has been kidnapped and they killed a young girl at her place. Not sure why they haven't killed Sunday yet, but they will soon. They took off north from her house in a black truck."

"With skulls? That's Big Dog's truck," DeMax said. "Don't sound like they're going to his place, though, it's the other way. I have my Harley. I'll catch up."

CHAPTER 13

Big Dog wheeled up to a big iron gate and punched the entry numbers. The gate opened, he drove through and it closed behind him. He stopped in front of a three-story mansion. Two men carrying automatic weapons rounded the corner then slowed down when they saw it was Big Dog and Biggen.

"Bring her along," Big Dog said. "Let get this over with."

Big Dog rang the doorbell and a tall elderly man in a tuxedo opened the huge metal door. Inside, a spiral staircase ran up to the third floor. Paintings by famous artists adorned the walls and a maid placed fresh flowers on a table in the foyer.

They walked over to double ten-foot mahogany doors with guards standing in front. Big Dog tapped on the door. A voice from inside said "Come in."

A gray-haired man wearing a purple robe was sitting at a desk with his back to them, watching a game show on a wall TV. He was in his seventies with thin gray hair, a ruddy-looking and wrinkled face with a short gray beard. He turned around and stared at Sunday.

"So, you're Detective Sunday?" he said.

"Yeah, and who the hell are you?"

"Your real father," he said.

"Not to me," Sunday said.

"When you and Necessary started giving me trouble, I found out you were adopted by Robert Verves in '89 and that your mother was Maria Estella," he began. "She was taking care of my children then and I was poking her every day. Ramirez talked your mother into stealing a million dollars from me when you were two years old. Maria told the midwife I was your father and then she told me. I gave you life, now I have to take it away like I did your mother. I wanted to see you in person before I got rid of you for good."

"I'd kill you if I could," Sunday said, trying to jerk free from Big Dog and Biggen.

He laughed. "I see you have the same fire in you as I do. Untie her, Biggen, and let her sit down."

"She'll run," Big Dog warned.

"Then shoot her," he said.

Biggen untied and sat her down, keeping a hand on the back of her chair.

"Would you like some wine or cheese?"

Sunday only stared at him.

"Might as well have some, it will be your last meal."

She continued to sit in silence.

"I can see you're not having any thoughts of living past today. So be it. Big Dog, when you dispose of her, drop her body off at police headquarters. I want them to see it."

"Be a pleasure, boss," Big Dog said. Biggen stood her up.

"They'll get you," Sunday said. "You wouldn't make a pimple on my daddy's ass."

"Take her away." He swung his chair back around to watch TV.

As Sunday was being marched out, gunfire burst through the mahogany doors and the two guards fell on the floor dead.

Mecana rushed in and put a bullet between Big Dog's eyes before he could fire a single shot. Darcie cut Biggen down as the SWAT team mowed down four more guards running into the mansion, then took a defensive position in case anyone else entered.

Sunday picked up Big Dog's gun and pointed it at the old man as he was reaching into a desk drawer.

Mecana pushed her away and emptied his Glock into the man. He fell facedown onto his desk, his hand still in the drawer.

Sunday ran to the desk and kicked him out of the chair. He fell to the floor with a chrome-plated .45 in his dead hand, blood oozing out from under him. She kicked him again and again, cussing and crying.

Darcie came to her and put an arm around her. "It's over, Sunday. He's dead."

"Why did you do that Mecana?" Sunday asked. "I wanted to kill him."

"I know, but it would have been something you had to live with forever."

"That's why I wanted to do it."

"Right now, sure, but maybe not later," Mecana said.

"Where did all the cops come from?" Sunday said.

"We called Simon for a SWAT team," Darcie said.

"How did you find me?" Sunday said.

"We'll talk about it later. We're going to take you home with us for now." Mecana said.

CHAPTER 14

After hours of coming back down to the reality of things, Sunday regained her composure. DeMax explained to her that he saw Big Dog's truck sitting in the driveway of the mansion when they were searching for her and he knew it was the only one like that. It had real gold flakes in the paint and was worth over three hundred thousand dollars. He said Big Dog drove it to flaunt his money, but it ended up costing him his life and saving hers.

"Maybe I'm alive for a reason I don't know about yet," Sunday said. "I wanted him dead but I think you may be right, Mecana, it was better you killed him than me."

Mecana's phone rang – it was Verves calling. "I knew I could count on you," he told Mecana. "You saved my daughter's life."

"I had a lot of help, Chief, and Sunday was the main one who figured it out. We got lucky in finding her. If you have any doubts about what she thinks of you, don't. She was ready to die for you and Valisa."

"Simon told me what happened. I know what a bulldog you are and that you never give up. She might have died like Angela without you and Darcie."

"She's past all that now," Mecana said. "She knows it's time to move on."

"Yeah it is, isn't it," Verves said.

"She's making arrangements to have the murdered teenage girl buried in the local cemetery and see to it that her family gets the reward."

"I'm so proud of her," Verves said.

"We all are," Mecana said.

"Thanks again," he said. "See you soon."

"Yeah take care of yourself," Mecana said.

Mecana and Darcie decided to go to Austin together. Darcie wanted to meet Amanda and get to know his kids. They invited DeMax along but he was getting ready to pop the question to his new girlfriend Mabre.

Sunday never spoke again about her biological father, a man known only as Mr. Money. Detectives were still searching for information on the man.

Simon Necessary finally retired as Chief of Homicide and took over Angela's restaurant. He changed the name to Angela's House.

Verves' health improved and Sunday started dating Eddy Hanson. They had worked together on several cases and plus, his desk was next to hers at the police station.

Twisted justice was the answer to the past and the present.

THE END

About the Author

John L. Lansdale was born and raised in East Texas. He is married to the love of his life Mary. They have four children. He is a retired Army reserve Psychological Operations Officer and a combat veteran with numerous medals and awards. Past roles include inventor, country music songwriter and performer, and television programmer. He produced and directed the Television Special "Ladies of Country Music." He has also produced several albums in Nashville, hosted his own radio shows and won awards for producing and writing radio and television commercials.

Lansdale was a writer and editor of a business newspaper. He has worked as a comic book writer for Tales from the Crypt, IDW, Grave Tales, Cemetery Dance and several more. He co-authored the Shadows West and Hell's Bounty novels with his brother Joe R. Lansdale. He is also the author of Zombie Gold, Horse of a Different Color, Slow Bullet, When the Night Bird Sings, Broken Moon, The Last Good Day, Long Walk Home and several more titles soon to be released.

THE MECANA SERIES by John L. Lansdale
#1 - Horse of a Different Color
#2 - When the Night Bird Sings
#3 - Twisted Justice

Titles by John L. Lansdale
Slow Bullet
Long Walk Home
Zombie Gold
The Last Good Day
Broken Moon
Kissing the Devil
Shadows West (with Joe R. Lansdale)
Hell's Bounty (with Joe R. Lansdale)
Boy and Hog (Short Story)
Boy and Hog Return (Short Story)
Emergency Christmas (Short Story)
Tales from the Crypt (Comic Series)
That Hellbound Train (Graphic Novel)
Yours Truly, Jack the Ripper (Graphic Novel)
Shadow Warrior (Graphic Novel)
Justin Case (Graphic Novel)

Follow the author online at
www.bookvoicepublishing.com
www.twitter.com/mybookvoice
www.goodreads.com/johnllansdale
www.facebook.com/bookvoicepublishing

SLOW BULLET
a novel
John L. Lansdale

In this timely novel, Clark McKay, a retired Army Special Forces Colonel, has developed a drinking problem after losing his wife and son in a car accident, as well as from the nightmares of his Vietnam days. And he's not getting any younger. In spite of his problems, he is determined to find out who murdered his best friend and his friend's wife.

A Washington D.C. detective refuses to believe McKay has found the murderer, a former CIA operative and arms dealer who murdered McKay's friend because he discovered the truth behind the assassination of JFK – preventing President John F. Kennedy from ending the Vietnam War.

McKay learns there are CIA documents his friend hid that will prove the conspiracy to be true. His search for these documents takes him all over the world. On his journey, after wading through all the corruption, McKay is brought to the conclusion that he may have to resort to murder if justice is to be served. What happened over fifty years ago is still with us today. In fact, many still doubt the "lone gunman" theory put forth by the Warren Commission. Could there truly have been a conspiracy to keep JFK from ending the war?

Truth and fiction make an interesting mixture in this fast-paced and entertaining novel. There are always those who escape justice. One hand washes the other, unless you have someone like Clark McKay who is willing to pay the ultimate price.

HORSE OF A DIFFERENT COLOR
a novel - Mecana Series #1
John L. Lansdale

"…the author's innate ability to spin a complex tale painted with vivid characters and intense suspense provides readers with a well-paced book that they may find difficult to set down."
– Amazing Stories

Someone is murdering and mutilating young women in a Dallas suburb, using the same techniques as a case down in Houston the previous year.

When the second body is found, it seems the killer has moved his hunting grounds to the Dallas area.

As the body count rises, Detective Thomas Mecana – a divorced fifteen-year veteran of the Dallas Police Department – is assigned to the case.

He prides himself on always getting his man, but his tried-and-true methods of the past are not working.

To make matters worse, his supervisor assigns him a new partner, a young officer who has never before worked a murder case.

Add in two teenage daughters creating problems at home, and a boss threatening to fire him at work, and Mecana's life begins to unravel as he hones in on his suspect.

With hard work, and some luck, Mecana and his partner discover a most-unusual serial killer case with murder in its very genes.

They discover some evidence is so strange and unbelievable, it might be best left alone.

Checkmate.

WHEN THE NIGHT BIRD SINGS
a novella – Mecana Series #2
John L. Lansdale

Shortly after solving the horrific Mutilator serial killer case, Thomas Mecana and Darcie Connors are on the trail of a new suspect.

On the inaugural day of their own private investigation firm, the two detectives meet Candy Kane - a lascivious Dallas socialite who offers them a small fortune in exchange for protection.

A former patient of her psychotherapist husband has been trying to settle old scores by threatening Mrs. Kane' life. And he's not the only one out for vengeance.

With an ever-growing suspect list, Mecana must toe the line between friend and foe.

Each action leaves them sitting in the crosshairs of those wanting to claim the Kane fortune.

One wrong move could mean the end.

BookVoice Pocket Stories
Short Stories by John L. Lansdale

BOY AND HOG

In the deep woods, anything can happen.
A group of white-collar workers with a hand-drawn map
trek into the wilderness for a hunting expedition.
But out here, will they be the hunters or the prey?

BOY AND HOG RETURN

While searching for a missing hunting party, two game
wardens stumble onto a grisly scene hidden deep in the
woods. With backup on the way, will the wardens survive
the wait, or will unexpected visitors send them to an early
grave?

EMERGENCY CHRISTMAS

This heart-warming short story tells the story of the
Albright family at Christmastime, and the guest who
surprises them just in time for the holiday.
Along the way, the Albrights discover sometimes crisis can
bring a family even closer together.

LONG WALK HOME
a novel
John L. Lansdale

Ten-year-old Trenton O'Rourke's life was changed forever during the summer of 1944. He and his family lived on a fading farm like many others in the small town of Angel Point, Mississippi. With family members fighting in World War II overseas, and rising racial tensions back home, what was normally a routine summer turned into a nightmare of murder, loss, trying to cope with hard times to survive and surprise learning experiences of growing up. Trenton's life would have never been what it was had it not been for a chance encounter with someone nobody expected.

Keep your eyes peeled for

THE LAST GOOD DAY
and
BROKEN MOON

Two all-new Westerns from
John L. Lansdale and BookVoice Publishing

For questions, comments, reviews, or to contact the author, email:
bookvoicepublishing@gmail.com

<u>Follow us online at</u>
www.bookvoicepublishing.com
www.twitter.com/mybookvoice
www.instagram.com/bookvoicepublishing

BookVoice
Publishing

www.ingramcontent.com/pod-product-compliance
Lightning Source LLC
Chambersburg PA
CBHW051710180726
48283CB00004B/1288